SCARRY WORD BOOK
My House

Illustrated by Richard Scarry

Hamlyn
London · New York · Sydney · Toronto

House Building

Rabbit is making a house.
She is making it out of sand.
Pig is making a house.
He is making it out of bricks.
It takes a long time to build a brick house.
Pig will have to work very hard.

Here is Pig's brick house, finished at last.
Pig has a visitor today. Can you see who it is?
Look on the balcony — it's Squeaky Mouse!

Point to:

roof	smoke	car
chimney	door	doorstep
mouse	window	shutters

Houses

A house made of snow and ice is called an igloo.
A house on a boat is called a houseboat.
A house in a tree is called a treehouse.
A tall, narrow house in the city is called a townhouse.

Can you point to a
castle?
Long ago, some
people built their
houses inside castle
walls.
Do you see a very
modern house with lots
of glass?
It is called a
bungalow.

The Kitchen

Here is the Pigs' kitchen.
They do all their cooking here, except on warm summer days, when they have a barbecue outdoors.

Can you see:

taps
teapot
apple
dishwasher
colander
bottle

washing machine
spoons
tin opener
refrigerator
sink
plates

saucepan
soap
toaster
cupboard
lettuce

Baking

The Pigs are in their kitchen,
making gingerbread men.
Father Pig is mixing the
dough.
One little Pig is rolling out
the dough.
Another little Pig has cut the
dough with a cutter.

Point to:

stool	apron	dough
saucepan	jug	flour
baking tin	rolling pin	eggs
mixing bowl	lid	egg beater
oven gloves	bottle of milk	frying pan

11

Can you see:

tulip
bird
worm
trowel
fork
flowerpots
lilies of the valley
watering can
dandelion
violets
bird-house
morning-glory

daisies

hollyhock

dandelion

tulips

violets

In the Garden

Little Rabbit likes working in her garden, watering the flowers.
Can you point to the bird-house in Little Rabbit's garden?
The mother bird is bringing some food home for her babies.
What do baby birds like to eat?

morning-glory

lilies of the valley

Outdoor Games

Look at all the children playing in the garden.
Can you count them?
There are nine children.
How many are playing on the swings?

Can you see a kitten playing with a top, and another kitten skipping?
There are some piglets playing marbles and one digging in the sand-pit.
What is the fox doing?

Point to:

marbles	skipping-rope
spade	sand-pit
top	rings
ladder	roller-skates
swing	bucket

In the Playroom

Sometimes the children play
indoors.
There are lots of things to do.
Do you like to build things or
play with cars?
Point to the game you like best.

Point to:

electric train
teddy bear
doll's house
toy car
rocking-horse
robot

17

The Bathroom

Look at the happy
elephant in the bath!
He is having a good time.
Do you enjoy having a
bath?

Point to:

glass	toothpaste
soap	tooth-brush
tap	bath
towel	curtain
basin	elephant

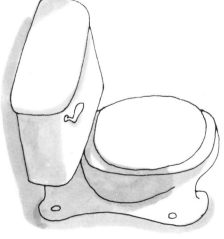

The Bedroom

To bed, to bed! It is late.
The moon and stars are
shining in the night sky.
Little Elephant snuggles
under the covers.
His mother is going to
read him a story.
Have you got a favourite
bedtime story?

Can you see:

bed   book
stool   moon
stars   glass
mother   pillow

20

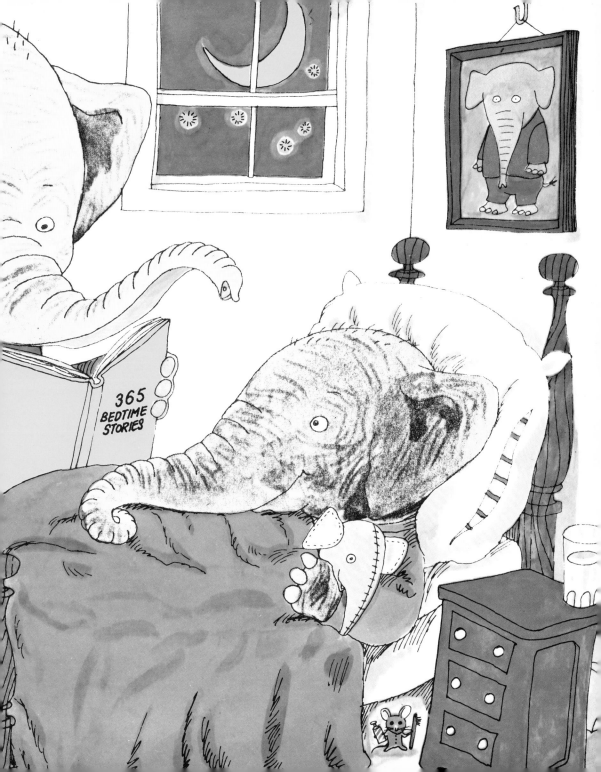

Good Night

It is bedtime for all the little animals.
They have all had a bath and put on their pyjamas.
Can you see someone wearing green pyjamas?
Who has blue pyjamas?
Two of the little animals are wearing nightgowns.
Can you point to them?
What colour are their nightgowns?